Tubby
and the
Lantern

by Al Perkins
Illustrated by Rowland B. Wilson

BEGINNER BOOKS   A Division of Random House, Inc.

Tubby was a very small elephant.

Tubby was almost small enough
to fit under a bed.

Almost.

But not quite.

But Tubby was a very good size
for a pet.
He belonged to a boy
named Ah Mee.

Ah Mee and Tubby
lived in a town
by the Rolling River.
Their house was on
the Street of the Golden Lanterns.

Everyone on the street
made paper lanterns.
They were lovely lanterns.
They floated in the air.

Ah Mee's mother and father
made the best lanterns
of all.

Ah Mee helped them.
Tubby helped Ah Mee.

Ah Mee and Tubby
made frames for the lanterns.
They made them out of wood.

They stuck gold paper
to the frames.

They made candles.
They put the candles
inside the lanterns.

10

Then they painted the lanterns.

Every day the family went across
the Rolling River to the market.
They took the lanterns there
to sell.

But today was a special day.
"Today is Ah Mee's birthday,"
thought Tubby.

"I must make a birthday
present for him."

Tubby took all the candles
in the shop.
He melted them in
an ENORMOUS pot.

Tubby made all the little candles
into one ENORMOUS candle.

Tubby took all the wood
in the shop.
He made
an ENORMOUS frame.

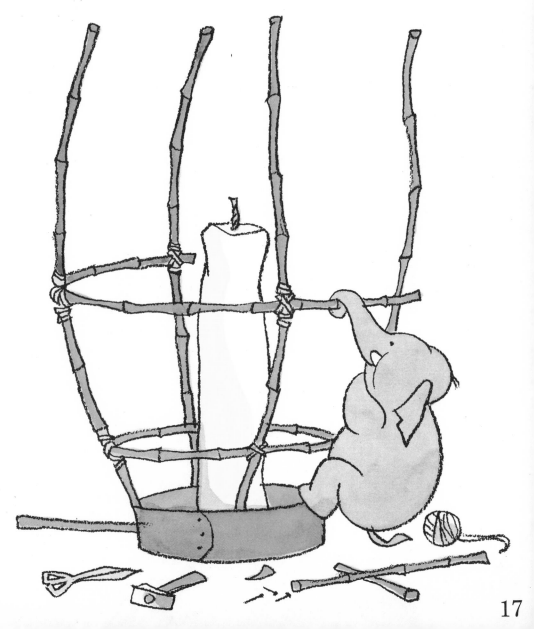

Tubby took
all the golden paper
in the shop.
He stuck it
to the frame.

He took all the paint

in the shop.

Then he wrote

"HAPPY BIRTHDAY AH MEE"

in ENORMOUS letters.

19

"What a lantern!"
thought Tubby. "This is
the most beautiful,
most ENORMOUS
paper lantern in the world."

Tubby lit the candle.

The big lantern began to
fill with hot air.

It began to float!

Tubby grabbed it.
But the lantern went up,
and Tubby went up with it!

Up over the river went
Tubby and the lantern.
They floated over the town.
They floated over the market.
They floated right over Ah Mee.

Ah Mee looked up.

He saw the lantern.

He saw "HAPPY BIRTHDAY AH MEE"
painted on it.

And he saw that Tubby was in trouble.

"Hold on Tubby," called Ah Mee.

"I'll save you!"

He grabbed a lot of little lanterns.

He tied them all together.

Up went the little lanterns.
And up went Ah Mee.

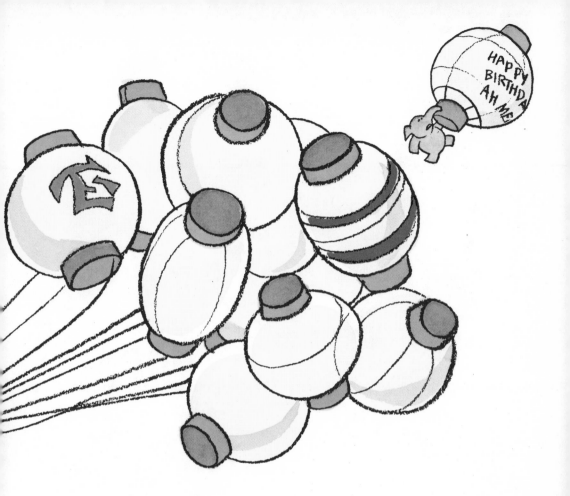

Up and up went Ah Mee.

But then something went wrong.

His candles began to go out.

His lanterns began to fall.

Tubby reached out as far as he could.
And just as Ah Mee
fell past him...

...Tubby caught him.

33

The birthday lantern floated on all night.

It floated over the mountains.

It floated over the sea.

"Thank you, Tubby," said Ah Mee.
"It is the best birthday present
I ever had.
But how will we get down?"

Then the sun came up.

And something new went wrong.

The big candle was going out.

The birthday lantern was falling.

Tubby and Ah Mee looked down.
They could see two boats.
The lantern was falling
into the sea between them.

"Catch this," shouted a sailor.

He threw them a rope.

Tubby caught the rope.

The sailors pulled them in.

"You are not safe yet," said a sailor.
"Those pirates are still after us.
If they catch us,
they will toss us all
into the sea."

"I know what to do,"
said Ah Mee.
"Help me move
my birthday lantern."

"Quick! Put the lantern
over the smokestack."

"Tubby, tie our lantern to the boat."

The lantern began to fill
with hot smoke.

The lantern began to float again.

The lantern went up.

And the boat went up with it.

Up into the sky it floated.
It left the pirates far below.

The lantern floated over the sea.
The lantern floated over the hills.
Ah Mee and Tubby looked down.
"We're almost home," said Ah Mee.
"I see the Rolling River."

"Turn off the smoke," called Ah Mee.
The hot smoke stopped coming
out of the smokestack.
Very slowly
they all came down.

They landed in the Rolling River
right next to Ah Mee's house.
Ah Mee and Tubby took
the birthday lantern off the boat.

That night everyone came
to Ah Mee's birthday party.
The party was two days late.
But they had it anyway.

And the next day was Tubby's birthday.
Ah Mee knew just what
to give him.

Ah Mee got a hammer and some nails.
He got some wood.

And he made a bed.

He made it so he could sleep on top.

And he made it so
Tubby could sleep underneath.

Now every night Ah Mee and Tubby
sleep in this bed.
And every night they dream
the same dream.

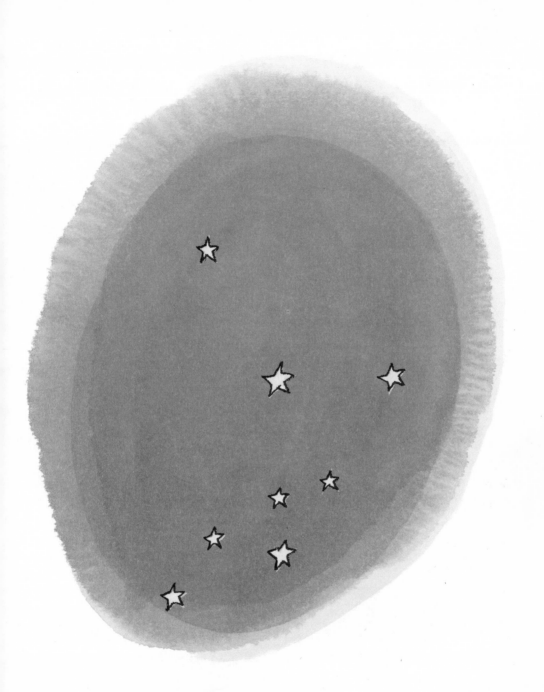

In their dream…

...they float away again
in the most beautiful,
most ENORMOUS
paper lantern in the world.

But they always
come back home...
safely...every morning.